REACHING

For Carly, Denby and Emily, always within reach — JAS
For Sasha and Liam — SM

Text © 2011 Judy Ann Sadler
Illustrations © 2011 Susan Mitchell

Kids Can Press acknowledges the financial support of the Government of Ontario, through the Ontario Media Development Corporation's Ontario Book Initiative; the Ontario Arts Council; the Canada Council for the Arts; and the Government of Canada, through the BPIDP, for our publishing activity.

Published in Canada by
Kids Can Press Ltd.
25 Dockside Drive
Toronto, ON M5A 0B5

Published in the U.S. by
Kids Can Press Ltd.
2250 Military Road
Tonawanda, NY 14150

www.kidscanpress.com

The artwork in this book was rendered in watercolors.
The text is set in Sabon

Edited by Debbie Rogosin and Sheila Barry
Designed by Julia Naimska

This book is smyth sewn casebound.
Manufactured in Shen Zhen, Guang Dong, P.R China, in 3/2011 by Printplus Limited.

CM 11 0 9 8 7 6 5 4 3 2 1

Library and Archives Canada Cataloguing in Publication

Sadler, Judy Ann, 1959–
Reaching / Judy Ann Sadler ; illustrations by Susan Mitchell.

For ages 0–3.
ISBN 978-1-55453-456-2

I. Mitchell, Susan, 1962– II. Title.

PS8587.A2394R43 2011   jC813'.6   C2011-901073-9

Kids Can Press is a l'OrUs™ Entertainment company

REACHING

Written by
Judy Ann Sadler

Illustrated by
Susan Mitchell

Kids Can Press

Mama is reaching
Lifts Baby up high

She swings him and sings him
A sweet lullaby.

Daddy is reaching
To kiss Baby's nose
He laughs and he tickles
Plump tummy and toes.

Sister is reaching
Wants in on the huddle
More kisses and tickles —
A fun family cuddle.

Grandma is reaching
Scoops Baby from Mum
She dips him, they dance
She rocks him, they hum.

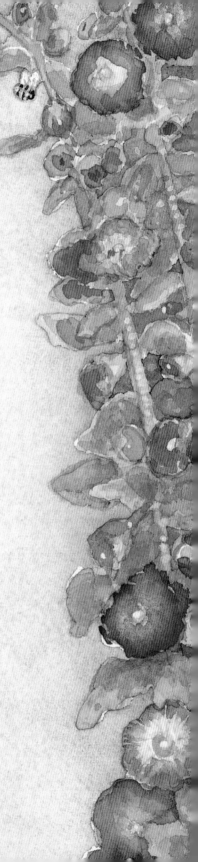

Grandpa is reaching
His arms become reins
He plays horsey with Baby
— They do it again!

Puppy is reaching
She just wants to play

She licks Baby's face
Then scampers away.

Oma is reaching
To kiss Baby's cheek
She covers her eyes
Then laughs and says, "Peek!"

Opa is reaching
His glasses are gone
Baby is grinning
He has glasses on!

Cousins are reaching
Hold hands all around

Rosies and posies
We all — fall down!

Great-gran is reaching
For their favorite book
Baby is wriggling
He can't wait to look.

Auntie is reaching
For both Baby's hands
She holds on, he wobbles
And now Baby stands!

Uncle is reaching
He's hovering near
Baby is walking —
They all clap and cheer!

Now Baby is reaching
For everything new

Looking and pointing —
There's so much to do!

Soon Baby will reach
For the moon and the stars ...

But not quite yet, Baby,
For now you're still ours!